The Widow's
Daughters

The Widow and Her Daughters

and other classic fairy-tales

Retold by Fiona Waters

Illustrated by
Gail Newey

BLOOMSBURY
CHILDREN'S
BOOKS

For Penny, with love

First published in Great Britain in 2000
Bloomsbury Publishing Plc, 38 Soho Square, London, W1V 5DF

Copyright © Text Fiona Waters 2000
Copyright © Illustrations Gail Newey 2000

The moral right of the author has been asserted
A CIP catalogue record of this book is available from the
British Library

ISBN 0 7475 4719 X

Printed in England by Clays Ltd, St Ives plc

10 9 8 7 6 5 4 3 2 1

Contents

The Seven Sisters

A story from the Native American Ojibwa Tribe

It was a fine summer evening and the young warrior, Silver Otter, decided to go fishing in the lake near his tepee. The last fingers of sunlight were glancing through the tall fir trees that fringed the lake and the whippoorwills were flitting

across the water, calling softly to
each other. The warrior pushed his
canoe out on to the water and cast
his net over the side. Then he sat,
letting his thoughts wander as dusk
slowly settled over the calm waters
of the lake.

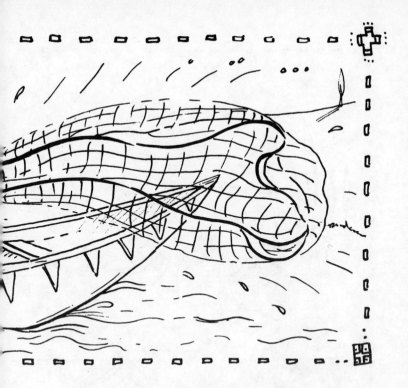

He gradually became aware of a
distant sound of singing, but oh
such heavenly singing! He had
never heard anything like it in his
life. He stood up in the gently
rocking canoe and looked all about
him. The fireflies were dancing over

9

the water and bats were swooping in and out of the trees but nowhere could he see any other human being. The singing grew louder and it seemed to be coming from above him. He looked up into the inky black sky and to his amazement a great basket was dropping slowly down on to the shore. He pulled up his net, and sat still as a possum watching the descent of the basket.

It came to rest on the glittering white sand by the water's edge and out stepped seven beautiful young maidens all dressed in white with long hair, black as the midnight sky, falling down their backs. They were

all singing the same haunting song
that Silver Otter had heard floating
down from the sky. They linked
hands and, still singing, began a
stately dance across the sands. Silver
Otter had never seen such graceful
dancing and he was enraptured and
so captivated by their voices that he

began to sing too. Instantly the
dancers fled back to the basket and
before Silver Otter could pick up
his paddle to row back to the shore,
the basket rose up into the midnight
sky and disappeared from his
sight.

All through the next day, Silver

Otter could think of nothing else but the beauteous maidens of the previous night and he vowed to hide somewhere on the shore that evening in the hope that the magical basket might descend once more from the sky. As the sun was setting, he made his way to the lake and crouched carefully under the thickest of the fir trees. As it grew darker, he held his breath lest the slightest sound give him away.

His patience was rewarded. The air was filled with the sound of high clear voices and the basket slowly descended to the land once more. This time the maidens were wary,

they looked all round before
stepping out of the basket. But soon
they were dancing again as the
water lapped gently on the shore.
Silver Otter thought they were even
more beautiful than before and in
his eagerness to get closer, he

stepped on a twig which broke with a loud snap. Instantly the maidens tumbled into the basket and Silver Otter was left on the shore looking up into endless night. Of the basket there was no sign.

The next day Silver Otter was wild

eyed with lack of sleep and all he
could think of was getting close
enough to the maidens to capture
one so he could make her his bride.
Long before sunset he crept down to
the water's edge and hid himself
behind a large rock. He waited and
waited. The moon came up and rose
high in the sky and still there was
no sign of the basket and not even
the faintest sound of sweet singing.
Still he waited and waited. It was
the dead of night and not a creature
was stirring. No fish ruffled the
water of the lake, no creature rustled
in the undergrowth and still there
was no basket. Silver Otter was

close to despair. He feared he had
frightened the maidens away for
ever and that he would never see
them again.

And then he heard the sound he
had been waiting for. Far away he
caught the gentle sound of voices
and slowly the basket descended

from the sky. But as it came to rest
he could see the maidens were very
afraid. They all huddled in a corner,
looking around nervously.

'Is it safe do you think?' said one
and her voice was like crystal water
running over a stone.

'Perhaps the sound we heard was

just the wind in the trees,' said another and her voice was like the gentle whirr of a butterfly's wing.

'Or perhaps it was a small animal in the rushes by the water's edge,' said yet another and her voice was like the gentle cooing of doves.

Silver Otter watched and did not move a muscle and eventually the maidens ventured out of the basket but they were still very cautious and the eldest, who was the most beautiful, kept looking over her shoulder. One by one they began to dance and soon their voices took up their beautiful song. Silver Otter let out a soft breath and began to creep closer. He had his eyes on the eldest and he waited until she was so close to him that he could hear her heart beat, then he leapt to his feet and clasped her to him. She shrieked in terror and all the other maidens rushed to the basket which began to rise slowly into the sky. They called to their sister, struggling to escape from Silver Otter, and leant out of the basket, their arms reaching out to her. But the basket rose silently into the sky and Silver Otter was left with the maiden, who was weeping bitterly.

He spoke gently to her and promised he meant no harm. He

told her he had fallen in love with her and wanted to look after her for ever. He promised her flowers and honey, warm moccasins and a soft bed under the stars. Gradually her tears ceased and she looked up at Silver Otter standing by her side.

He did not look so very threatening
and he was smiling at her so she
spoke to him.

'I cannot stay on earth with you.
I am a daughter of the Sun and
Moon and with my sisters am one
of the stars you call the Pleiades. My

father the Sun will be very angry
that I have come to earth to dance
as he has forbidden us ever to leave
the skies. Please let me return
before daybreak and then he need
never know that I have disobeyed
him.'

Silver Otter was heartbroken at
her words but he took her by the
hand and said,

'I am afraid of no man. Let me
speak to your father and perhaps I
can persuade him to let us be
together.'

The maiden shook her head sadly
for she did not think Silver Otter
would be able to move her father

but she saw that the young warrior
was brave and yet gentle so she
agreed to wait until the next evening
when her sisters would return in the
basket.

When the basket was lowered to
the ground, the six remaining sisters

looked at Silver Otter with great fear
but the eldest told them not to be
anxious. She promised to explain
everything to their father and so
Silver Otter rose up to the heavens
in the basket with the seven star
sisters.

The Sun was indeed very angry, not only with his star daughters for defying him, but also with Silver Otter for daring to think he might be able to marry one of his precious children. He raged and raged and grew very hot indeed but eventually he could see that the fine young warrior did indeed love his daughter and so agreed to their being married.

'But you may never again return to earth and my other six star daughters likewise may never again visit the lake to dance in the moonlight. One earth husband is quite enough!' he roared.

Silver Otter very bravely spoke up and said,

'But may we not visit sometimes? I should like my fellow warriors to see my beautiful wife.'

The sisters were horrified by his presumption but eventually the Sun

laughingly agreed that Silver Otter
and his bride could visit the earth
now and then as long as they
promised always to return. And that
is why sometimes when you look at
the Pleiades you will only see six
star sisters. You will know then that

Silver Otter and his star bride are down here on earth, singing and dancing on the shores of the lake.

The Widow and Her Daughters

A story from Scotland

There once lived a very poor old
widow and she had three daughters.
Indeed the daughters were the only
thing she had for she lived in a wee
cottage with just a small kale yard
out the front. And she didn't even
have the kale to make herself and

her daughters a pot of soup for
every day a great grey horse came
up and ate all the plants.

Now winter was coming and the
widow was at her wits end. The
horse was eating most of the kale
and the chill wind was blowing in

through the rough walls of the
cottage. The widow's eldest lassie
said to her mother,

'Let me sit out in the yard
spinning and then when the great
grey horse comes I will drive him
off.'

And so the lassie did as she promised and ere long the great grey horse came up and began to eat the kale. The eldest lassie leapt to her feet and began to hit the horse with the distaff from her spinning wheel but to her alarm it stuck fast to the horse and as he moved away, the lassie was forced to run alongside him. On and on the horse trotted with the lassie running quite out of breath by his side until they reached a queer round hill with trees along the bottom and wild crows cawing in the trees. The great grey horse stopped and cried out,

'Open up, open up, green hill. I

have brought the widow's eldest
lassie.'

A low door slowly opened up at
the foot of the hill and the horse
walked in, taking the lassie with
him. As soon as they had passed
through the door the great grey

horse turned into a handsome
young man right before the lassie's
very eyes. And handsome is as
handsome does, the young man
fetched a bowl of warm water and
washed the lassie's poor tired feet
and gave her food and drink. Then

he took her to a fine big room with a huge soft bed and left her for the night.

In the morning the handsome young man appeared and gave the eldest lassie a huge key ring which he said had keys to all the rooms in the great house beneath the green hill. She could open all the doors she could find except the heavy wooden door at the end of the darkest corridor. He bid her eat whatever she wished from the kitchens and asked only that she have a meal ready for him when he returned in the evening.

The eldest lassie set off to explore

the house and she found it was vast.
She wandered into endless rooms,
all richly furnished and very
comfortable, with long tapering
candles burning in every one. Ere
long, she reached the heavy wooden
door at the end of the darkest

corridor and found there was only one key left that she had not used.

'Why should I not open this door too?' she mused to herself. 'No one will ever know.'

So she slid the key into the lock and opened the wooden door. She

found herself in a vaulted chamber piled high with gold and treasure and sparkling jewels. She went from corner to corner, trying on some of the gorgeous necklaces and bracelets and rings and time fairly sped by. She suddenly realised with a great start that the young man would be home soon and she hadn't prepared any food for him so she ran back into the dark corridor and pulled the great wooden door closed behind her. She ran into the kitchen and hastily began to make a great pot of soup. As she chopped the potatoes and cabbage she heard a soft mewing and there by her feet

stood a wee black cat. Great was her
astonishment when the cat spoke to
her!

'Mistress, you have done that
which you were forbidden to do.
My Master will be angry with you.'

Well, the eldest lassie was not fond
of cats and unimpressed by even a
talking one so she shooed the cat out
of the kitchen with an angry shout.
The wee cat looked over her
shoulder and said,

'You have done that which you were forbidden to. Mind my words when my Master comes home.'

By and by the handsome young man came back. He was not very impressed with the thin soup that the eldest lassie had prepared for him and asked her what she had been doing all day. She said she had been busy all day and had only just finished all her work.

'And did you go into the room with the great wooden door at the end of the darkest corridor?' he asked quietly.

'Indeed I did not,' said the eldest lassie firmly (she had her fingers crossed behind her back).

But the young man asked to see her feet, and oh! there stuck to her foot was a shiny golden coin so he knew she had been lying. He bundled her up in a great sack and

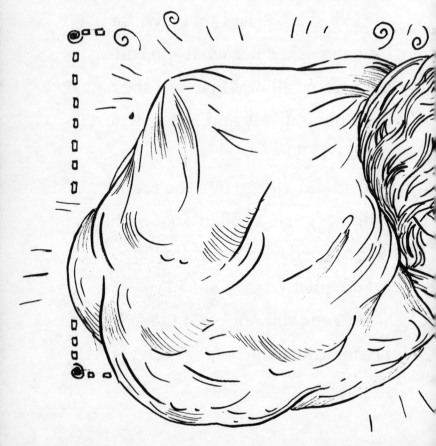

stuffed her into an empty corn
barrel. Then he gave the wee black
cat a saucer of milk.

The next day the widow's second
lassie was sitting in the yard with
her sewing when the great grey

horse came in the gate and began to eat the kale. The lassie jumped to her feet and hit the horse but her thread stuck fast to the horse's side and she too was forced to run off after him just like her sister before her. Ere long they reached the queer round hill and the horse said,

'Open up, open up, green hill. I have brought the widow's second lassie.'

And all happened just as before. In the morning the young man gave the second lassie the same instructions, and I am sorry to say she was no better than her sister before her. She too went into the

great treasure chamber and spent
hours looking at all the glittering
jewels. She too ignored the wee
black cat and only produced a poor
meal of over-cooked potatoes for the
young man when he returned. She
too denied having been in the

forbidden room but when the young
man looked at her feet there was a
shiny gold coin and he knew she
had been lying. He bundled her up
too and put her in the same barrel as
her sister. Then he gave the wee
black cat a saucer of milk.

Now the poor widow only had one daughter left. But she was a canny lassie and she promised her mother that she would not only get rid of the great grey horse but would also find her two sisters. So she waited for the horse and instead of striking him, she hid by the yard fence and followed when he left after eating the last of the kale. She ran silently behind him all the way to the queer round hill and saw him enter and change into the handsome young man. He had known she was behind him all the time so bid her welcome and gave her food and drink, and showed her to the fine

big room with the huge soft bed. In the morning he gave her the same instructions as her sisters. And her curiosity was as great as her sisters so she too opened the great wooden door and entered the treasure chamber. But wealth had no attraction for her so she closed the

door and went into the kitchen to prepare a meal for the young man. There she met the wee black cat, purring by the hearth. She stroked the cat and put down a saucer of milk for her. The cat lapped up all the milk and then looked at the youngest lassie.

'Now, my lassie, in thanks for your kindness I will tell you a thing or two. Your sisters are in that corn barrel and you must leave them there for the time being. There is a gold coin stuck to your foot which you must remove before my Master returns. Now you must prepare him a good meal and perhaps we can all be saved.'

And the wee black cat curled up and went to sleep again. The youngest lassie cooked a wonderful rich stew that smelt marvellous and baked a great blueberry pie. Then she waited for the young man to return.

He ate the stew and had two great helpings of the pie before he asked the lassie what she had been doing all day. She crossed her fingers and said she had been so busy that she had never had a moment to leave the kitchen, and when the young

man asked to see her feet the coin had gone so he believed her. So she passed another night in the huge soft bed.

She was woken by the wee black cat licking the end of her nose with a rough rasping tongue.

'Now,' said the wee black cat, 'you can save my Master from his enchantment. When he arrives tonight as a horse you must throw a plaid over him and beat him with a rowan branch. Then you will see what you will see,' and the wee black cat curled up and went to sleep again.

All day the lassie made her preparations. She took a heavy tartan plaid from off the settle and hid it by the door in the side of the queer round hill. Then she cut a great branch of rowan off one of the trees and placed it over the threshold. And she waited. The sun dipped behind the hill and she heard the sound of galloping hooves. The great grey horse arrived and the youngest lassie threw the plaid over his shoulders and struck him with the rowan branch. There was a great whoosh and then there was nothing to be seen. Horse, plaid, rowan branch had all disappeared and all that was left was a small pile of ash on the doorstep. Then the lassie heard the young man's voice, and he was laughing and crying at the same time. She turned round and there he stood and his eyes were clear and he said,

'Lassie, you have released me from an evil spell placed on me many, many years ago by an evil kelpie. I have riches enough to keep you for the rest of your days. Will you marry me, please?'

And the lassie said she would be delighted to marry him, not for the riches but because he was a kind man. And the only thing she could be persuaded to take from the house under the queer round hill was the wee black cat – and her sisters, of course!

Two Sisters and Their Caribou Husbands

A story from Greenland

Far off in the dark frozen North by
the edge of the sea, there once lived
two sisters and their brother. In the
summer days the sisters gathered
roots and the brother caught fish
which they would salt away for the
winter. Their life was harsh but they

knew no other and so they were
content.

When the sisters woke up one
morning it was so bitterly cold that
the sea was frozen so they decided
to walk across to the Western Rocks
where they hoped to find more

plants to eke out their meagre fare.
Waving goodbye to their brother
who was sharpening his harpoon,
they set off across the frozen sea,
striding over the ice in their great
fur-lined boots. They had not gone
far when from nowhere a great

wind rose and the ice began to break up and the sisters were carried far out to sea. The Western Rocks disappeared over the horizon and the sisters were in unknown and uncharted waters, and they were very frightened. But then the wind dropped as suddenly as it had arisen and the sisters found themselves on the shores of a strange island. No sooner had they set foot on the land than the ice floe that had carried them there melted without trace and in despair they cried aloud, thinking they would never see their brother or their home again.

The older sister was the first to recover.

'Dry your eyes, sister. We must use our wits to survive now. First we must eat,' and she took out the

wing-tip of a great gull that she
carried as a charm. She held the
feathers up to the sky and muttered
some words under her breath.
Straightway a huge salmon flipped
out of the water at her feet.

'There, my sister! Now we shall
not starve.'

They lit a fire and placed the
salmon on a smooth stone in the
ashes and soon there was the most
delicious smell wafting upwards in

the smoke. After they had eaten
they made camp as well as they
could and went to sleep.

When they awoke in the morning
two dark shadows lay across their
faces. Two seal hunters were
standing close by watching the
sisters, their kayak pulled up on the
shore.

One of the men smiled and said to
the sisters,

'Do not be afraid. We are very
happy to see you as what we most
desire in the world is to marry, and
here you are!'

As proposals go the sisters felt it
lacked grace but they were sensible

enough to realise that they would not survive very long in this strange land on their own so they scrambled to their feet and looked more closely at their future husbands. They were both tall and strong and seemed pleasant enough. And so the sisters were married.

For a time they all lived happily together. Each of the sisters produced a baby girl. They were delighted with their beautiful daughters and told them all about their home far across the sea. But the husbands were not pleased.

'Why have you only given us

girls? We need sons to help us fish
and hunt. We do not need
daughters,' and they grew morose
and silent.

Things did not improve and the sisters resolved to try to return home to their brother, far across the sea. They waited till the winter came and the ice covered the sea again. Now the husbands had nothing to do as they couldn't hunt seals so they went to friends where they passed the time dancing and singing. One evening when the singing was especially loud, the sisters stole away with their daughters wrapped tightly in their fur hoods. All night they walked and all the next day and another night and just when they thought they could go no further they

recognised the Western Rocks. They
walked just a little further and there
was their old home! And outside sat
their brother sharpening his
harpoon. He was delighted to see
them and thought their daughters
were enchanting and as they sat

round a warm fire eating, the sisters
told him all that had befallen since
they set out that long time ago. The
sisters told him how rich the far off
land was with plenty of salmon and
seals and caribou.

'Let us journey there in the spring

so we may replenish our stores for next winter,' said the brother.

The sisters were less keen for they feared their husbands, but the brother was determined and promised they would go armed with charms to protect them. And so as the days began to lengthen the brother prepared his biggest boat. He placed two charms within, a duck's wing and a scale from a salmon, and the sisters packed baskets with food for the journey. One morning the brother looked far out to sea and said,

'It is time, my sisters. Have courage, this time I am with you

and we will succeed,' and he
stepped into the boat with the
sisters and their daughters and the
whole family pushed away from the
shore.

They sailed and sailed and the
brother used his magic charms to

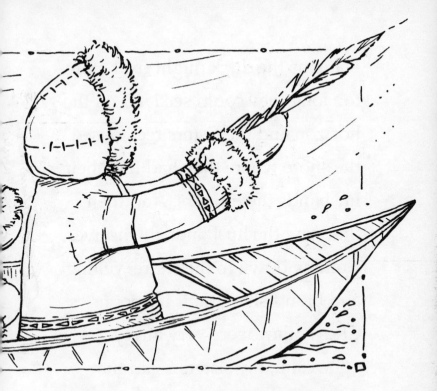

help the boat over the water. When
they needed to rest he held the
salmon scale up to the sky and the
boat moved gently through the
waves just as the fish might swim. If
he held the duck's wing up to the
sky, the boat skimmed over the

water as the duck might fly. Before too long they could see land on the horizon and the sisters recognised the shore where they had met their husbands the hunters. And then they saw the husbands themselves, running down to the shore, yelling and brandishing their harpoons. Clearly they were very angry.

'Be calm, my sisters,' said the brother. 'I will protect you.'

He drew a flask from his pocket and as the husbands raced up to the boat, the brother sprinkled water from the flask over them and straightway they were turned into caribou.

And the sisters realised to their
astonishment that their husbands
had been caribou in disguise.

'No wonder our husbands only wanted sons,' they cried and held their beautiful daughters even closer.

The brother spent many days hunting salmon and seals and caribou. The sisters dried and salted

the salmon, skinned the seals and
prepared caribou hides and soon the
boat was groaning under the weight
of all this bounty. When they could
pack no more in, the family set off
back home with enough provisions
to see them through the longest and

coldest winter. And who knows,
perhaps the husbands went too,
rolled up at the bottom of the boat!

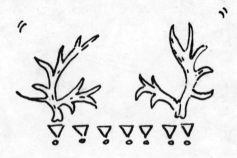